This special book
belongs to

_____

_____

D1275920

To children of all ages, all races, all cultures, all over the world,
all planets and especially for Victor (and Julia).– Javier Mariscal

To children everywhere who are celebrating the earth.– Kim Summers

This book was produced by Melcher Media, Inc., New York
Charles Melcher, Publisher
Kate Giel, Editor
Andrea Hirsh, Production Director
Designed by Estudio Mariscal

Library of Congress Catalog Card Number: 98-71565
ISBN 0-8109-4176-7

Copyright © 1998 by Melcher Media, Inc. and Estudio Mariscal
Illustrations copyright © 1998 by Estudio Mariscal

Published in 1998 by Harry N. Abrams, Incorporated, New York

All rights reserved. No part of the contents of this book may be
reproduced without the written permission of the publisher or the
copyright holder.

The type was set in Mundo Romana

Printed and bound in Hong Kong
by C&C Offset Printing Co., Ltd.

Harry N. Abrams, Inc.
100 Fifth Avenue
New York, N.Y. 10011
www.abramsbooks.com

Señor Mundo
and me

A Happy Birthday Story

By Javier Mariscal
Written by Kim Summers

Harry N. Abrams, Inc., Publishers
Produced by Melcher Media, Inc.

Lizzie had the birthday blues.
She perched on her lookout
over the bay,
with only her Starfish for a friend.
She didn't see the sky turning pink.
She didn't see bright waves prancing below.
Lizzie was too busy
feeling sorry for herself to look.

Tomorrow was her birthday.
There was no one to celebrate with her.
She was stuck.
Spending her summer in a yellow house
on a dull deserted island, where there were no kids.
Just parents. (Two ever-busy scientists.)
And a giant computer.
Some birthday!!

That night her mother said,
"Lizzie! Tomorrow's your big day."

"We'll have an island birthday,"
 said her father.
"Coconut cake and mango ice cream!"

"And I suppose the computer will sing
 Happy Birthday?" said Lizzie.
"I can hardly wait."
 And she stomped off to bed.

The next morning Lizzie felt worse.
"We're running away," she said to Star.
"We'll go exploring, then they'll be sorry."
She typed a note on the computer.
"Adios!! Bye Bye!" she said. "We're off."

Suddenly someone spoke. "Happy birthday, Lizzie."

She looked at the computer.
There was only her note.
She looked at the screens on the wall,
their window on the world.
Something blue and green
was glistening there.
It was talking to her.

"Who are you?"
  asked Lizzie.

"Guess,"
  said the voice.

"You look
  like the world,
  but you can't be,"
  said Lizzie.

"I am," said the voice.
"I'm a whirl-around
  twirl-around
  home for living things.
  Señor Mundo at your service!"

"What an elegant name!"
  said Lizzie.

  Señor Mundo winked.
"An elegant name
  for a magical place," he said.
"Where are you going?"
  asked Señor Mundo.

"We're running away," said Lizzie.
"It's my birthday
  and there's no one to celebrate."

"No one?" said Señor Mundo.

"No one that matters," said Lizzie rudely.
"My friends are home, or at camp.
 Not stuck on a deserted island
 with their parents and a computer."

"Hmmmmmm," said Señor Mundo.
"Take a look. I'm a big place.
Where would you like to go?
I have mountains, prairies,
cities, and countries."

He twinkled and twirled,
sparkled and whirled s-l-o-w-l-y
so Lizzie could glimpse
his villages, towns, oceans, and bays,
jungles, forests, rivers, and streams.
As he spun,
pelicans flew,
flowers opened,
whales sang . . .

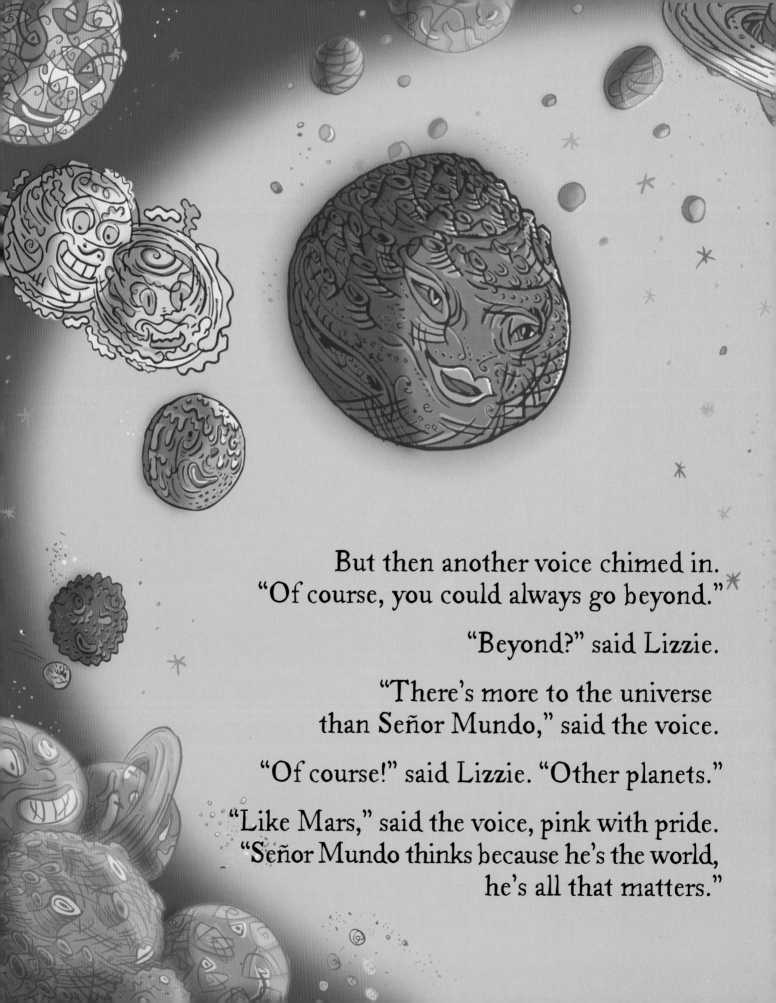

But then another voice chimed in.
"Of course, you could always go beyond."

"Beyond?" said Lizzie.

"There's more to the universe
than Señor Mundo," said the voice.

"Of course!" said Lizzie. "Other planets."

"Like Mars," said the voice, pink with pride.
"Señor Mundo thinks because he's the world,
he's all that matters."

"But humans can't live on Mars,"
  said Lizzie.

"Señor Mundo can make magic, if he will," said Mars.
"Look beyond," Mars coaxed . . . .
"Why not sail into space? Visit me.
  Have a real adventure.
  That's the way to celebrate your birthday!"

  The other planets chimed in.
"I may be small," said Pluto,
"but I'm worth a visit."

"I have the biggest halo,"
  said Saturn.

"Yes, he wears it round his middle,"
  jeered Venus.

  But Lizzie said,
"Mars sounds marvelous!
  Red is my favorite color."

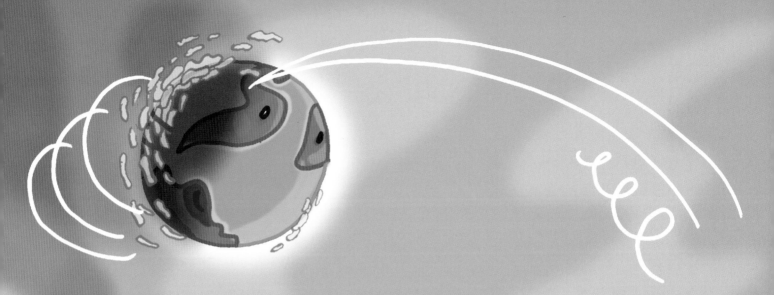

"I WIN!" bragged Mars with a smirk.

"Maybe," said Señor Mundo.

"But how will I get there?" asked Lizzie.

"It's your birthday," said Señor Mundo.
"I'm a mover of mountains. A maker of magic.
Have you seen my spider webs?
Tasted fresh tomatoes? Heard spring peepers?
You want to go to Mars? EASY!"

And he swirled a quick twirl.
Lizzie and Star shot into space.
Star peered over the side of his bucket.
And wished he hadn't!

"Adios," said Señor Mundo. "Happy Birthday!"

Mars was not like anything Lizzie had seen before.
Rocks and craters glowed sunset red.
Sharp shapes and hard edges sprang up
like sand sculptures.

Soft clouds clung to the canyons.
The cold was biting. The wind was sharp.
Ice caps glittered in the distance.

Dry riverbeds made patterns
on the rocky floor.
And then there was dust.
Dust that painted the planet red.
Dust that covered
the windblown dunes.

"Eeeerie," said Lizzie with a shiver
to Star. "No sign of life."
But Star was silent.
Stiff and frozen in his bucket.

"Oh!" wailed Lizzie. "Why did we come?
How can we leave?
What will we do?"

And then like a wish with wings,
Lizzie spotted something sparkling with light and life.

It was inching slowly up. Coming close. Closer.
Was it him? Could he come? Would he come?
After she was so eager to leave Earth?

"Señor Mundo to the rescue,"
said Mars with disgust.

"Proud to be here!"
Señor Mundo replied.
"You had your chance.
Now it's my turn!"

"You heard me wishing," said Lizzie,
gazing at the lifeless land.
"Look at poor Star, frozen in his pail."

Slowly a soft yellow ray warmed her face.
The ice in the pail melted.
Star stirred.
A cloud of mist began to rise.

"Climb aboard quickly!" said Señor Mundo.
"I'll lend you a cloud. Ride your wish home."

"Happy birthday!" said Mars with a sneer.

"Adios!" said Lizzie.

Star didn't wave goodbye.
Together they rode into space.
Down … down they dropped.

From forests, jungles, lakes, and shores, parrots, gulls, cockatoos, and flamingos flew up to sing Lizzie and Star home.

Below penguins flapped. Seals splashed. Turtles basked. Elephants trumpeted.

"We made it!" cried Lizzie.

"We're back!" said Star.

"Thank you, Señor Mundo," they said.

Lizzie looked around her with new eyes.

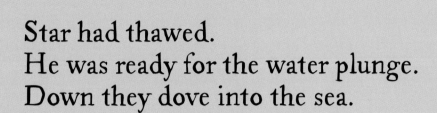

Star had thawed.
He was ready for the water plunge.
Down they dove into the sea.

Past the coral reef where octopus, fish in schools,
sea horses, crabs, and lobsters
whished by with a watery welcome.

Up on land, Lizzie and Star
found themselves in the small jungle
on their own tropical island.

After the chilling cold,
the sinister silence,
the lack of living things on Mars,
the forest was warm and teeming with life.

Leopards prowled, mynah birds squawked,
frogs croaked. Butterflies and birds
in rainbow colors flew with Lizzie and Star
as they made their way home.

After hugs and hellos at the yellow house,
Mom and Dad passed out funny hats,
paper masks, balloons, and horns
to the parade of animals and birds
who flocked behind Lizzie and Star.

Mom said with a wink, "No one to celebrate?"

Lizzie looked around and grinned.

"Not a soul!" said Dad.
"Have some mango ice cream, dear?"

Later, Lizzie stretched
out with Star.
They saw the sweep of the sky,
heard waves on the shore,
smelled the fresh green
of warm earth.

"Just think, we're part of it all,"
Lizzie said.
She took a deep breath
and smiled.
"Some birthday, Señor Mundo!"
she sighed, giving him a loving pat.
"You sure know how
to spin a party!"